THE EBONY STICK

BY

EARL DERR BIGGERS

Illustrated By Walter Briggs

British Library Cataloguing-in-Publication Data
A catalogue record for this book is available from the
British Library

Illustrations

Earl Derr Biggers

Earl Derr Biggers was born on 26th August 1884 in Warren, Ohio, USA.

Biggers received his further education at Harvard University, where he developed a reputation as a literary rebel, preferring the popular modern authors, such as Rudyard Kipling and Richard Harding Davis to the established figures of classical literature. Following in their footsteps upon graduating, he himself began a career as a popular writer, penning humourous articles and reviews for the Boston Traveler.

In 1913 he produced his debut novel The Seven Keys to Baldpate which was well received by the critics and public alike. George M. Cohen bought the theatrical rights to this work and it was eventually adapted into seven feature films, the first in 1915 and the last in 1983. Biggers compounded this success with his next two novels Love Insurance (1914) and The Agony Column (1916) and continued with his magazine contributions as well as writing plays. He enjoyed hits with the plays A Cure for Curables, which had a two year run in New York, and Inside the Lines, which ran for 500 performances in London.

While on holiday in Hawaii, Biggers heard tales of a real-life Chinese detective operating in Honolulu, named

Chang Apana. This inspired him to create his most enduring legacy in the character of super-sleuth Charlie Chan. The first Chan story The House Without a Key (1925) was published as a serialised story in the Saturday Evening Post and then released as a novel in the same year. Biggers went on to write five more Chan novels and all were licensed for movie adaptations by Fox Films. These films were hugely popular with several different actors taking the lead role of Chan. They were even a success in China where the appeal of a character from the country being the hero instead of the villain appealed to film-goers. Eventually, over 40 films were produced featuring the character.

Biggers only saw the early on-screen successes of Charlie Chan due to his death at the age of only 48 from a heart attack in April 1933.

THE EBONY STICK

AT nine o'clock on a bright June morning Clay Garrett, colored, intermittent sweeper and duster of the leading bank in a large Texas city, opened the heavy doors that led from the street into that most marble of bank interiors. Two minutes later—this being also part of the regular schedule—Major Tellfair, white-haired but erect, crossed the threshold, nodded to Clay and to the boys behind the bars, and passed into the office where he ruled as president. There he opened his desk, lighted a cigar, and began the perusal of his morning paper.

He had got no farther than the headlines of the first page when the door of his office opened and young Dick Merrill of the Silver Star Ranch came in. Merrill was covered with the dust he had collected on his ride in from the ranch that morning. Lighting his face was the Merrill smile, human and kindly, and it brought the major to his feet in hearty welcome.

"Sit down, Dick," he said. "Beautiful morning, ain't it? How are things out at the Silver Star?"

"The Silver Star's all right," Merrill answered. "But, say, I got a cablegram from Bob this morning." He explored a pocket. "Here it is. I wish you'd read it. Bob's in Italy—at a place called Rome—over there among them I-talians."

His tone was as disapproving as the pleasant Merrill tone could be. He deposited his husky length in a mahogany chair and waited for the major to adjust his glasses. The bank president noted the truth of Merrill's scornful statement as to Rome, and then read the message slowly:

Cable thousand dollars immediately. Care National Express. Keep matter under hat, Bob.

"What do you make of it, major?" Merrill asked.

The major smiled.

"It looks to me like somebody had annexed your brother's roll," he replied.

"That's how I figure it," Merrill said, also with a smile. "He's been in Italy less than a week too—they work fast, them boys. Bob had two thousand dollars small change, along with all his tickets, which he bought from this man Cook in New York. I hope they didn't clean him out of those too. Well, it serves him right for wandering off the range. He ain't got no business over on the other side."

The major cleared his throat.

"I don't wish to seem inquisitive," he said. "But I was utterly at a loss to understand your brother's sudden dash for Europe, particularly at a time when the nations over there are engaged in the most bloody and terrible warfare—"

"A woman," interrupted Dick Merrill. "It was a woman that done it. Maybe you remember her—Celia Ware—she used to sing at church concerts hereabouts a few years back."

"Ah, yes, I have heard her sing," said Major Tellfair reminiscently.

"You'll hear her again," said Merrill, "I reckon you don't pay much attention to such things, but old Bob sure was far gone on her. And she seemed to think a heap of him too."

"Naturally," nodded the major.

"But when it came to a showdown she picked her art. Wedded to music she was. Went over to Italy to get better acquainted with it. Bob got a letter from her 'bout a month back: wants to divorce her art now. Maybe it's grounds of non-support, maybe the war's upset her, maybe she just naturally loves old Bob—I don't know. Anyhow, she told him to come for her, and they're to be married over there: in Florence. Ain't that a devil of a sissy name for a town?"

"It's an Italian name, I believe," responded the major. "Miss Ware struck me as a singularly attractive young woman. I'm sure I congratulate your brother most heartily."

"Oh, Celia's all right," said Merrill. "How she'll pan out on a ranch I don't know, but she's a mighty fine girl, even if she did drag poor old Bob all them thousands of miles to Italy."

"We must send him his thousand," mused the major. "No man wants to be broke on his wedding day."

"Sure: dig into his account and send it along," agreed Merrill. "He's boss, and it's his money. Shoot it to him. Only I wish he hadn't been so all-fired brief. I wonder what happened. Bob's too childlike and simple to wander around among them I-talians. Somebody got to him. I wonder—oh, well—send him the money, major: I leave it to you."

The major promised to attend to the matter immediately, and Dick Merrill, still wondering, set out for the Silver Star Ranch.

There was a rumor in that Texas city to the effect that Major Tellfair was growing too old and forgetful for the position he held, and, unkind as this assertion sounds, subsequent events seemed to justify it. The gentle old president turned back for a moment to his newspaper. Shortly after he was interrupted by the cashier, who had an important matter to discuss. The cabled appeal from Bob Merrill slipped out of sight on his cluttered desk, and for two days the Texas ranchman waited forlorn in the city of Rome.

He might have waited indefinitely had not Clay Garrett, the aged negro custodian of the bank, been a devotee of that art which has made Caruso wealthy. On the third day following the visit of Dick Merrill to the bank, Major Tellfair entered at two minutes past nine in the morning to hear Clay giving a spirited rendering of a favorite song.

Fortunately for Bob Merrill, two lines of that song reached the ears of the major:

"Darling—Ah am growin' ol'—
Silver threads among the gol'—"

Silver! The Silver Star Ranch! Bob Merrill's cablegram! In an agony of remorse the old major rushed into his office, unearthed the message, and sent the thousand dollars speeding toward Italy. Then he returned to sit before his desk in humble and pathetic contrition, while the sneers of his enemies regarding his age and absent-mindedness filled his thoughts. He was a most unhappy man.

Perhaps he would not have been so unhappy had he known that by those two days of delay he had done Bob Merrill a most unexpected service. For he had caused the ranchman to break his sacred contract with Thomas Cook & Son to leave Rome on an appointed day and thereby enabled him—

But we are far, far ahead of the story. Offensive to the schools of short- story writing it must be when we confess that the incident already related bisects squarely the tale we have to tell. The most seemly thing to do then is to go back quietly to the beginning—back to that rainy Saturday morning when the little Italian liner slipped away from the fog-engulfed pier in the North River, New York, carrying Bob

Merrill ultimately to his ladylove, but first to the adventure of the ebony stick.

Though Celia Ware's letter of surrender warmed his pocket, there was a homesick twinge in the heart of the big ranchman as he watched the towers of Manhattan fade back into the mist. Little enough he had in common, it is true, with the great city of cabs and cabarets, but as the scene of his farewell to his own beloved land it suddenly took on, for him, a new and tender interest. The five thousand miles of restless water he was about to cross appalled him in prospect, and Naples, his destination, struck on his ears like the name of some new, unexplored planet. Nevertheless, like the true knight he was, where love led he followed. If you could have seen him there at the rail, broad-shouldered, handsome, with the look of one who would always he a boy at heart, you would not have wondered that in the letter now resting in his pocket, Celia Ware renounced forever her cherished career. In a hundred galleries abroad she had seen the figures of men great artists had thought worthy of their marble, and her waiting lover suffered in comparison with none of these.

A wall of fog had risen now between Merrill and the country he was leaving, but still he stood at the rail, lonely and staring. A noise at his elbow brought him round, and he saw standing behind him a neatly tailored young man with a face so friendly and smiling that his own smile at once returned.

"Some little disappearing act the old burg did this morning," said the young man, pulling his checked cap down on his head. "Now you see it and now you don't. This your first trip over?"

"First offense," Merrill confessed, "How about you?"

"My seventy-first crossing; actual count," responded the stranger with a bored air.

Merrill gasped. "Business, eh?" he inquired.

"Business," assented the other, a queer little look in his eyes. "As we're to be two weeks together on this hopeless old tub, we ought to get acquainted. My name is Henry Howard Fisher."

Two days Merrill had spent in Manhattan, and his heart was hungry for companionship. Quickly he revealed his name, mentioned Texas, the Silver Star, and suggested a drink.

"Sorry," said Mr. Fisher. "I don't touch it."

"Come and have a cigar then," Merrill ordered. It developed that neither did the abstemious Mr. Fisher smoke. Merrill looked him over again, a trifle suspiciously this time. Men were not made thus in the neighborhood of the Silver Star. But Fisher's face was frank and winning, and he was delighted, he said, to accompany Merrill to the smoking room for a chat.

Comfortably seated, Mr. Fisher regarded the ranchman thoughtfully while the latter made known his wants to a steward. Then with a some what satisfied air he took up, and showed himself a master of the waning art of conversation. They spoke of the war. Mr. Fisher touched lightly on the matter that was now taking him abroad. It seemed that a rich tract of land in the neighborhood of Naples, which he owned, had been atrociously taxed because of Italy's recent entry into the great conflict, and he was going over to adjust the matter. A terrible bore, said he, sighing. He inquired as to the route of Bob Merrill, and the ranchman explained how Cook, friend of tourists, had arranged everything in advance.

"Cook picked me up this morning after breakfast in New York," he laughed, "and he won't drop me until after dinner on the night of the 20th of July, when I land back in the North River. Tickets, hotels, everything bought and paid for, and, you might say, in my pocket."

Fisher laughed. "You might as well send your trunk," he said.

The satire, however, was lost on his friendly audience. Merrill took out a typewritten route sheet and read from it:

"Land Naples eight o'clock Saturday night, June 10, stop Grand Hotel du Vesuve; June 11, breakfast and lunch at hotel, take train Statione Centrally three o'clock p.m.

for Rome, dinner on train, arrive Rome seven o'clock, stop Hotel Quirinal—"

"You don't stay long in Naples," Mr. Fisher commented.

"Friend." replied Bob Merrill, "I don't stay long anywhere until I get to Florence. Expect to do a little sight-seeing on the return trip to Naples, where I get a boat back home. You see, Mrs. Merrill will be with me then."

And to this stranger he frankly told what took him abroad.

"Youth on the prow and pleasure at the helm," quoted Mr. Fisher delightedly. "It certainly is refreshing to find somebody going abroad on a happy errand in these war times." He looked Merrill over again. "By the way," he added, "have you been down to arrange for your seat at table, or did Cook do that for you too?"

This was something Cook had left to Merrill's own initiative, and Mr. Fisher accompanied him to the dining saloon on the errand. Thus it came about that the ranchman and the pleasant Fisher were seated side by side at the same table for the crossing.

The little dining saloon was crowded at that first luncheon, but it was the last time for many days that all its seats were filled. For it developed that the mist which engulfed New York was but the western fringe of a tremendous storm. For five days the liner struggled in the angriest of seas. One by one the passengers disappeared and were seen no more. Each night Bob Merrill's sleep was disturbed by his bright new steamer trunk rolling as the ship rolled back and forth, back and forth, across the floor of his narrow stateroom. Frequently he heard outside in the companionways the crash of chinaware as stewards carrying trays were hurled against the walls. It was a new experience for the Texan; he was awed by the power of the sea, but unafraid. And with a little group of the faithful he appeared three times daily in the dining saloon.

Fisher, hero of seventy crossings, was, of course, one of that group, and he complimented the ranchman on his digestion. In those five days, when the rain was on the sea and the liner almost helpless in the wash of the waves, their isolation brought them very close together. They began to know each other by their first names. To the man from Texas his new-found friend was more or less a mystery. Sometimes Fisher seemed very young to him; he looked again, and there were many marks of age on Fisher's face. Sometimes he thought the stranger the frankest of men; at others he discovered a sly look that worried him.

But Fisher's polished manner, his interesting fund of talk—which was but rarely of that tax on the acres of Italy which was his immediate worry— fascinated him as well as all the others aboard with whom the man came in contact. Fisher had a charming way with women; three children who were immune from the sickness worshiped him at sight. There was but one person on the boat— a little old lady who looked the sewing-circle but was a famous traveler—who seemed to find his courtly manners displeasing.

Often the ranchman tried to discover some business connection of his friend, but in vain. "You'll find a volume of my poems on sale at Brentano's in New York," said Fisher one day, and thereby became an even greater mystery to the Texan. Indeed, save for those acres in Italy, no earthly business seemed to hold him.

The fifth day the rain ceased, and the waves began to calm. A few of the suffering passengers crept cautiously on deck. "They remind me," said Bob Merrill to Fisher, "of old Jeb Peters, our town atheist back home, the first time he went into the Methodist church. Peters was willing to give the place a trial, but everything had to be just so."

That night the moon they had all forgot crept through the clouds and poured its silver on the sea. After dinner Bob Merrill sat in a deck chair, looking out over the tossing waters. He was alone with his thoughts, which were of the vast dimensions of the world in which he lived. For five days they had plowed on, seeing nothing save one small fishing boat. For nine more days, over three thousand miles of water, they were still to plow. In awe and reverence he considered these things: how the world was so much greater than he had ever dreamed, how the Silver Star back there in Texas was but an unimportant atom in God's huge scheme of earth and water!

Suddenly, through a port hole behind him, came the voices of two men in the lounge: "Well, well, well! Why, I got a brother in the paint business in Dubuque." And the answer: "Say, ain't it a small world after all." At this ridiculous interruption to his thoughts Bob Merrill threw back his head and laughed. And the little gray lady who looked so sewing-circle, striding by on her evening constitutional about the deck, paused before him, then dropped into the chair at his side. "It surely does me good to hear a laugh like yours," she said. "Would you mind telling me the joke?"

He told her, and she joined him in his mirth.

"A small world," she remarked scornfully. "I guess not. I guess I know. I've been traveling in it more than thirty years: just going on and on. The uneasy woman, boy, you see her in the flesh."

"Seems to me it's dangerous for you to travel in Europe now," said Merrill.

"I hope so," she answered. "Danger's great fun. My sister and I were stoned in Spain during the Spanish-American War. How Nellie did enjoy the thrill! She used to travel with me, Nellie did. Died last year in Australia, poor dear. I brought the body home, and then I started out again. It's lonely without her, but I can't stop. Got to go on. Russia, Turkey, China, the Philippines—all the countries you can name—I've been there. Can't stop. The uneasy woman. I'll die on the road."

With wonder in his eyes, Bob Merrill, the timid traveler, gazed at the frail little woman beside him. She leaned closer.

"Something I've been wanting to say to you," she went on. "Don't think me an old busybody, boy. You told me it was your first crossing. I only want to be of service to you. I've been on the road a long time. This—what does he call himself—this Henry Howard Fisher? You and he are pretty thick."

"I reckon we are," Merrill admitted.

"He's been on the road a long time too," the little woman said. "Lots of names he's called himself. I forget them now. But I've met up with him many times. What a splendid, what an inventive mind he has. What a magnificent crook he is!"

"Crook!" said Merrill, sitting up.

"Exactly," answered the woman. "Hard to believe, isn't it? Even after her ten thousand was gone, it was hard for my friend, Mrs. Markham, to believe. She'd read his poems. I have too: they're beautiful. It was hard for Joe Deming to believe. Joe was consul at Rio—gave this Fisher all his savings—five hundred. Why? Fisher asked for them: so pretty." She laughed. "I've seen many of them at work," she said. "Fisher is the best. Go on mixing with him if you like:

to know him is a liberal education. But sew your money up tight, boy, and laugh at him if he talks business. If you do that, there's no reason why you shouldn't mingle with a very charming man of the world at little cost to yourself. I'll be going on."

"Wait," cried Merrill. "I appreciate what you've done. I—"

"Don?t thank me—think," said the little old lady, and was gone.

Merrill thought. Had a man cast this slur on the honor of his new friend, he would have been quick and hot to defend him. But he saw in the eyes of this eccentric old lady nothing but sincerity and truth. She was no doubt quite right. She had been about a bit. She knew. His delightful companion of the decks and the saloon was nothing but a con man de luxe.

Later that evening, during a pleasant chat with Fisher in the smoking room, came his opportunity to make use of his knowledge. Fisher had been watching while the ranchman sipped a highball—liquorless and smokeless himself, as always. Suddenly he leaned across the table, and his face was as old and worried as Merrill had ever seen it, though he sought to keep his tone light.

"Bob," he said, "I don't mind telling you: I'm in a deuce of a hole owing to that land of mine near Naples. They've put a heavy tax on it—several thousand our money—and

16

I can't pay. The land's worth much more than that, but I'll lose it if I don't come across. I've been wondering—a first mortgage on it for the amount of the tax—could I interest you? We could run out and look the land over that morning you're to spend in Naples—"

He paused, for a most disconcerting smile had come upon the simple face of the ranchman. It was hardly what Fisher had expected.

"Just a minute, Henry," said Merrill. "You and me've been pretty good friends. Don't you go and spoil it all. Don't you go and try to sell me no option on Vesuvius. Nor any first mortgage on the dead city of Pompeii."

"What do you mean?" faltered Fisher, laughing, though his face grew a bit pale.

"Just what I say, Henry," replied Merrill cordially. "Friends, yes. But if it's business you want to talk, the bars are up, Henry, the bars are up."

"You question my honor—" began Fisher hotly.

"Sure I do," answered Merrill. "Don't get riled. Have a drink—if you've been off the stuff to impress me. Have a drink and let's talk about art, or cattle, or poetry. But real estate—say, Henry, whose land was you thinking of giving me a mortgage on?"

Fisher sat staring at him a long moment and then, making his decision, broke into a laugh.

"By Gad," he said, "I like you, Bob. I'm glad you're on: it relieves me of the stern necessity of lifting your roll. I thought I had to do it—and, gosh, how I dreaded it."

"Now you're talking." smiled Merrill. "I've got a letter of credit in my pocket for two thousand dollars, real money, along with my tickets and such. You've been trying for days to find out the amount: that's it. Now, Henry, you keep off. Let's be friends."

Fisher looked at him admiringly.

"You're a wise one," he said. "I didn't give you credit. I was fooled because you hadn't been about much. Nobody could do you. I ought to have known it. You're a wise one."

"You flatter me," Merrill answered, "but it would be foolish to deny it's music to my ears. Now that our cards are all on the table, we can go on being friends as before. Why not, Henry?"

"No reason," agreed Fisher heartily.

"I will have a drink if you insist. Yes, Bob, you've called me. You're a good judge of men, Bob. You're safe anywhere—" He paused a moment thoughtfully. "Most men are as easy as children, but you—"

Late into the night his flattery continued. Expanding, he told of some of those he had swindled; random examples of the many from Rio to Dawson City, from Hong Kong to Gibraltar. Bob Merrill listened. He felt that, as the old lady of the travels had predicted, he was gaining a liberal education.

The liner plodded on, into a world of sunny days and moonlit nights. To those who lived in that world the thought of Europe bleeding to death began to seem a nightmare and a delusion. The decks, the lounge, the smoking room, were crowded now with many men traveling on many errands. Still daily in each other?s company, the big clean ranchman and the hero of many shady deals spent much of their time. Fisher spoke no more of those mythical acres in Italy. His tongue was often oily in praise of Merrill as a judge of men; but mostly he confided, as in a friend he could trust, the thrilling tale of his exploits by land and sea. And Merrill, who ashore would have thought often of the police, listened and learned.

They touched one evening at Gibraltar, taking aboard several men, one or two of whom seemed not unknown to Fisher. At night, when the moon was high above the Rock, they sailed again, and there followed four days of the Mediterranean, with its waters now blue, now green, now purple; always lovely. Happy as was Merrill's errand in Italy, he grew to dread the day when he must step ashore. The little liner, with its endless odor of rubber companionway coverings, had grown to seem like home.

On the morning of the fourteenth day of their journey Fisher asked to see the type-written page that held Cook's directions for Merrill, and he studied it for several minutes.

"Our paths may cross again," he explained, handing it back. "It surely has been great to know you, Bob. A real friend—one of the few I've known. If I'd had somebody like you at the start, I might never have gone into this rotten game."

Merrill put the list back into his pocket. He said nothing about meeting Fisher ashore. Though already dazed at thought of the strange country he was about to enter, it seemed best to him that he and Fisher should part forever at the pier. He was sure Celia would not approve of his new friend. He was not so sure that he himself would approve of him—on shore.

Late that afternoon some clouds he had been admiring in a brilliant sky developed into mountain tops, and the bay which is said to be the end of human endeavor lay dead ahead. Breathless, for his life in the open had made him sensitive to the beauty of hill and sky and water, Bob Merrill stood at the rail. All the thrill that Columbus had got from the sight of our rock-bound coast, Italy was paying back to the American at that moment.

Into his vision crept the hill of Posilipo, the low island of Capri. Then Vesuvius, crowned with its wreath of smoke, looking as the steel engravings had promised it should look.

And finally the city of Naples, its white villas climbing from the water's edge up toward the gorgeous sky. Below Merrill the steerage, with true Latin abandon, cheered and wept. They had come home again. The little Italian doctor came and stood at Merrill's side. His eyes glowed, and he pointed.

"See," he cried. "See, signor. That little patch of the white at the foot of Vesuve. That is my town: the town where I was born. Not in two years have I seen it. I go there to-night."

Merrill stood, trying to realize that in this glittering, unreal landscape men could point out a spot as home.

The liner slowed down and took aboard passengers from a small launch that flew the Italian flag. The ranchman hurried below; it was time for dinner, but, like the others he could eat little. However, Cook had commanded, so he made the effort. Then he went to his stateroom for the last time, to gather his hand baggage and tip his wistful steward. He was on the point of returning to the deck when the door of his stateroom opened suddenly and Fisher rushed in. His face was white; he trembled. He closed the door and leaned against it. "Bob," he cried, "I'm scared stiff. I'm sorry to have you see me this way. But I can't help it. I had to see you again."

"What's up?" Merrill asked.

"On the doctor's launch," gasped Fisher. "A woman—wife of the first secretary at the consulate—she was in Kyoto three years ago. I got next to the consul there for some real money. She's come aboard to meet friends. I think she saw me."

He paused, very shaky.

"I get this way," he apologized, "at the thought of arrest. They've never got me yet. But it's with me all the time, the fear: it makes my life hell. And when there's danger—like now—I feel all gone inside. You see, Bob, I'm a pretty poor thing after all. Not a man like you. I pretend, but, God, I'm afraid." He shuddered. "You won't see me again," he went on. "I'm going back in the second class, and go ashore with them. Maybe she didn't notice me; maybe I just imagine. But before I go, Bob, I want to say good-by and give you a little present. Something to remember old Fisher by."

He held out a walking stick, handsome, of ebony, with a very large gold handle, made in the image of an elephant.

"Take it," he went on quickly. "Keep it to remember Fisher by. I've carried it for years. I want you to have it."

"Why, I—" began Merrill. He saw that the stick was an expensive one. "I don't know that I ought to—"

"You mean because I haven't gone straight," cried Fisher, hurt.

"Not at all," said Merrill. "Thanks, Henry. I'll keep it. Thanks."

"A present from Fisher," whined the other. "A gift to the only man he ever met that he couldn't swindle. For that's what you are, Bob: the shrewdest, wisest man I ever struck. Keep the stick—and good-by."

He held out his hand. Merrill took it.

"Good-by, Henry," he said. "If you ever decide to go straight—good luck."

Fisher mumbled something and slipped out. With a look about to make sure that he had forgotten nothing, Merrill opened the door and followed. In his hand he carried the ebony walking stick; it was indeed a beautiful gift, and he looked down at it with pride. The gold elephant of the handle was very large, but not too large for a hand that had for ten years branded cattle in Texas.

Merrill went on deck. Dusk had fallen, and the stars were twinkling above the unlovely old warehouses along the waterfront. Like an ungainly lover sidling up to the lady of his choice, the liner was making clumsy efforts to dock. On the pier where they were shortly to land a black mass of people waited.

The ranchman stepped to the rail. Down below the waters were cluttered with small boats bearing venders of fruit and flowers. In one leaky craft a band of daring musicians twanged guitars and sang divinely "O-o-o solemia—" And there, faint in the dusk, were the villas, white and climbing; Vesuvius, with its eternal menace and its eternal romance, and over all the stars. Saturday night in Naples! Bob Merrill's heart beat fast. Truly, this was a land to come to in search of one's beloved.

The liner docked, and a gangway was dropped at an angle of forty-five degrees to the pier. Before the passengers could go ashore their baggage trundled down into that now howling mob and off through many hands to the customs. Bob Merrill watched with misgivings as his trunk was carried through the crowd. His heart sank, for he knew he must follow and rescue it from excitable little men who did not speak his language. Landing in Italy began to have its serious side.

Then he remembered the stick in his hand. A gift to a man who could not be swindled. Was he such a man, he wondered. He hoped so. He was still hoping when some one gave him a shove down that steep gangway, and the next thing he knew he was in Italy.

First to greet him was Cook's man, his blessed English voice rising heavenly above the clutter of a strange tongue. Merrill was rescued from the loudly raving hotel runners, and soon landed with surprising ease in the lobby of the Hotel du Vesuve.

That night he walked with the crowds on the Via Roma, amid the dandies, the cabbies with their eternally cracking whips, the laughing signorinas. Head and shoulders though he was above the little men of this country, they awed him with their babble. Meekly he submitted to their picturesque extortions. He felt lonely, lost, overwhelmed.

And those delighted Neapolitans were quick to realize his state of mind. Dazed Americans had once been no novelty, but scarce they were in these war times, and the more to be cherished. Bob Merrill was a babe in their woods, and they made the most of him. Many hands were stretched out in impudent demand for his pennies, and as he filled them all he grasped his ebony stick the tighter, smiling grimly when he remembered what was given to him.

The next afternoon a member of the band of forty thieves, disguised as a cabman, landed him at the station, and he left for Rome as per the promise he had made to Cook. He reached his destination at dusk, and the capital city was a revelation to him. The street of his hotel was as modern as Texas; crowds thronged it, gazing into the lighted shag windows, gathering at the doors of the moving-picture theatres. Street cars clanged down it. To one who had got his ideas of Rome from a picture of the Colosseum by moonlight, all this was startling. He was given a room looking out on the Via Nationale, and all night long the rattle of trolley cars broke in upon his sleep. Yet just behind his hotel the ruins of Nero's time lay white beneath the moon, and across the famous Tiber the great dome of St. Peter's stood guard.

He awoke next morning from his disturbed slumbers a happy man. By evening he was to gaze again into the eyes that had so agitated his bosom in far-off Texas; he was to hear that voice which had been raised to such melodious effect in a dozen church choirs. Celia was lovely, she was feminine, she was his.

He had just finished shaving when there came a knock at his door, and without ceremony a bellboy ushered a stranger into his room. He stepped Into the bedroom to find a small, swarthy Italian. with fierce mustache and shifting eye, waiting for him.

"Hello," said Merrill. "Who are you?"

"My most profound apology," said the stranger, "that I must thus disturb you. But it is of the greatest importance. I am in the service of the Government. You wish my credentials?"

He handed over stamped and sealed documents, and Bob Merrill stared helplessly at the unfamiliar script.

"Can't make 'em out," said the ranchman as he gave back the impressive bundle. "But I suppose you came to look at my papers. Go as far as you like." And he produced his passport.

"Ah, yes." The Italian read. "This tells you are an American, signor."

"You bet I am," Merrill answered. "One of the few left. I guess that's all, eh?"

The Italian shrugged his shoulders and walked slowly about the room, glancing at Merrill's possessions. Suddenly he wheeled, dramatically.

"If you are an American, signor," he cried, "how comes it that you serve Italy's enemies as a spy?" Bob Merrill had heard it was the common fate of travelers to be suspected, and he smiled pleasantly. But his heart sank. In this odd land of strangers he felt more than ever lost and alone could he make himself understood?

"Nonsense, Tony," he said genially. "Somebody has been handing you a fake tip."

"Somebody has made it known," the man answered, "that you carry papers of the utmost importance. I must search, signor."

"Search and be damned," the ranchman laughed. "I suppose it's your regular business. But make it quick, for I've gut a date with a breakfast downstairs."

He stood at the window while the little man stooped over his trunk, hastily overturning the contents. At home, among his own kind, he would have taken the stranger by the scruff of the neck and deposited him elsewhere. But when in Rome—

"Nothing to it, Tony," he smiled. "You're wasting time. There's my valise. See -innocent as a babe—that's me."

The Italian had paused. His eyes were on a corner of the room, where stood the ebony stick. He stepped over and took the gold elephant of the handle in both his hands. It came off, and from a hollow in the wood the emissary of the Government removed a thin roll of paper and held it up before Merrill's startled eyes.

"So, you carry nothing, eh?" The Italian spread the papers out on a table. Merrill saw that the topmost sheet was covered with crosses, waving lines, writing. "What is this? A map of the Champagne district in France: of trenches, of the distribution of forces. Information for Austria, a country with which Italy has been at war a month and over. Signor, you are under arrest!"

Merrill passed his hand before his dazed eyes.

"Look here, he said, "I don't know anything about this. That stick was given to me: a present from a friend."

"Signor, the weakest of stories is that—"

"But it's the truth."

"You will have the opportunity to explain later. But I advise that you find some story more plausible. It matters little, however. You are captured completely. Prison, signor, and—perhaps—the firing squad."

"Prison nothing. It would take a hundred like you to put me there."

"Then the hundred shall be found."

"I'm leaving for Florence this afternoon. I've an appointment there: with a lady." Merrill faced him helplessly.

"Let us hope the lady is not too charming," sneered the other. "It will be many weeks before you see her—if ever. Do not keep me waiting, signor."

Merrill strode to the window. So Fisher was a spy now and had made use of him. It was plain enough. Somewhere along the line a confederate was to have relieved him of the stick. He looked out on that foreign scene that had made him so childishly helpless even before he was in trouble. He would be taken where few spoke his language, and his explanation was weak in any tongue. It was incredible. It sounded poor even to his own ears. Prison would surely follow. He recalled a line in a play he had seen: "Italian prisons are devilishly uncomfortable." Meanwhile Celia would wait, frightened, woeful.

"Come, signor," urged the little man.

Suddenly into Merrill's mind flashed a statement made to him several times by Fisher in the course of his tales of graft. It was to the effect that no Italian official was above a bribe, rightly offered. He turned and looked the Italian in the eye.

"See here," he said, "you've saved your country's honor. That's enough, ain't it? What will you get by dragging me off to jail? Nothing. If you could see your way clear to letting this matter drop I might make you a very handsome present."

The man drew himself up to his full height, which was little.

"You insult," he said, "me, my position, my Government. It is unworthy of you. Come, signor."

"Five hundred dollars," said Merrill.

"No; I'll put it in your money: it sounds more. Two thousand five hundred lire—a neat little sum. Go out of here and forget what you've found and it's yours."

The man smiled.

"My price it is cheap, in your eyes," he said. "No, signor—many times no." He came closer. "Ten thousand lire," he added softly. "Not a centesimi less."

"Two thousand dollars," Merrill answered. "You've got your nerve. Take me to jail." He put on his hat. "I suppose I can communicate with the embassy." he said.

"If you like," agreed the Italian. "Three other men of your nation, caught as you are caught, have communicated. It does little good. There are negotiations— what you call red tape—a long time is taken. Meanwhile you wait in prison."

Merrill paused. He cursed Henry Howard Fisher under his breath. He thought of Celia—of her happy, eager letter that had been waiting for him at Naples.

"All right," he said. "Come over to the bank with me and I'll cash in on my letter of credit. I'd like to fight this, but I can't afford to be held up now."

They went out into the sunlight, the Italian carrying the ebony stick. At the Banca d'Italia Merrill showed his passport and canceled his letter, receiving in return ten Italian notes, each good for a thousand lire, along with a little small currency that represented the difference in exchange. Had there been an American behind the bars of that bank the deal might have fallen through. But here, too, everything was foreign, strange. They returned to the street.

"Here, you merry little grafter," said Merrill, "take your money, quick, before I brain you. You caught me with the goods, and no mistake. How about that roll of plans?"

"See," said his companion. "To Italy I am true. The plans, I destroy them."

And, standing there on the street corner, he tore into shreds the papers Merrill had been carrying in the ebony stick.

"You might give me the cane," suggested Merrill. "I'd sort of like to keep it, as a souvenir."

"A thousand pardons," the Italian answered. "It is not good you should carry it. A stick of this style: it is better in my hands than in those of—a spy."

And he walked away down the street, gayly twirling the stick in his hand.

Merrill stood looking after him, chagrined that he had been so easy, yet knowing in his heart that he had done the only wise thing. To be dragged into court as a spy, particularly when the evidence was so hopelessly against him, would have been unthinkable at this time. Money came quickly at the ranch, and Celia's company weighed against ten thousand lire easily tipped the scales. He hoped, however, that he could keep the matter from the boys at the Silver Star.

He set out for his hotel. If he had felt helpless in this foreign land before, he felt vastly more so now that his pockets were empty and his credit gone. He searched for funds, and found only his tickets and a few lire that would hardly last the day out. Back at the hotel he sent his cable to Dick asking for another thousand. Fortunately he was able to charge it, though this was not included in the scheme of Cook. And he knew that now he could not leave Rome until his money came. The hotel porter explained to him that owing to the difference in time the cable would probably reach Texas at an even earlier hour than that at which it was sent, and predicted that the answer would come back by evening at the latest. Merrill cheered greatly to hear this. But we have seen how that cablegram was swept into the discard on the desk of Major Tellfair. The hour came when the ranchman was due by his promise to Cook to start for Florence, and there had been no word from Texas. He was compelled to send Celia a telegram stating that he was delayed. All the next day and the next he waited, fuming, wondering. Cook's arrangement served him no longer, and his bill at the hotel was mounting. He sent Celia frequent telegrams, charging them on that bill. He was a worried man.

But, fortunately for the ranchman, Clay Garrett was moved on the morning of the third day to sing "Silver threads among the gold," and thus wake the major to his forgotten duty. At three in the afternoon the money reached Rome, and Bob Merrill, much relieved, paid his bill at the hotel and took the four o'clock train for Florence.

On that ride to the lovely city of his happiness he was crowded into a second-class compartment along with five army officers and what appeared to be an Italian honeymoon. The afternoon was warm, the quarters cramped, and the scenery along the way not what he had been led to expect of Italy. But at the end of that journey waited Celia, and he was content to sit and dream, while the soft language of the country, being squandered on all sides of him, lulled his senses. In the corridor outside the compartment walked many Romeos, stopping now and then at the door, after the Italian custom, to stare impudently at the lady who was within.

For three hours Merrill sat in his cramped corner, and then he decided to become one of the walkers in the corridor. He strolled up and down several times, stretching his legs. His path led him past several first-class compartments at the farther end of the car. One of these had its door closed, its curtains drawn. Pausing reflectively outside, Merrill caught a glimpse beneath a curtain not quite down of two gray and natty spats. They seemed somehow familiar. Going the Italians one better, he deliberately stooped and looked into the compartment. Lolling at his ease in a corner, the sole occupant, he beheld Mr. Henry Howard Fisher!

Smiling with joy over his discovery, Merrill thrust open the door and came abruptly into the presence of his erstwhile friend. At sight of the ranchman Fisher's eyes narrowed, but he leaped to his feet in cordial greeting.

"By Gad," he cried, "if it isn't Bob Merrill. I thought you had left for Florence several days ago. Your tickets from Cook—"

"I had an accident," said Merrill.

"So sorry. What happened?"

"Those little plans you gave me, Henry, along with the ebony stick. Of course you haven't heard—"

"Plans—what plans? Sit down, Bob." Fisher thrust Merrill down upon the seat opposite. "Hot in here, isn't it?" He took off the light-gray duster he was wearing to protect his faultless attire from the stains of travel. "Don't you notice it—devilish hot? What was the accident, Bob?" And he carelessly threw the duster on the baggage rack above his head. His aim was good but luck was against him. For Bob Merrill's eyes, following the duster, saw that from one end of it there still protruded a large gold elephant, the head of a handsome ebony stick!

For some Seconds, with Fisher's frightened gaze upon him, Bob Merrill sat staring at the stick. And now at last into his simple, unsuspecting mind there flashed the truth regarding the game that had been played on him. Hot anger swept into his heart. Fisher, watching, one eye on the door, saw and shuddered.

"W—well?" stammered Fisher at last.

"Well?" repeated Merrill sharply. He turned his eyes from the stick. "Well, Henry, you're shivering again. Like you were on the boat that last day. All sort of gone inside, eh? Afraid—God, you're afraid."

"What are you going to do?" Fisher demanded.

"I don't know," replied Merrill. "I'm a slow thinker, Henry. Be patient with me. Give me time. Blamed if your teeth ain't chattering. Buck up, be a man. You make me sick to look at you. The police haven't got you yet."

"You can't prove anything," Fisher cried. "Not a thing—"

"I know it," Merrill answered. "Come, Henry, try and be a man." The anger was gone already; the smile returned. "You ought to know I'm not the sort to run sniveling to the police. I'm just as afraid of the jabbering bunch as you are. I couldn't explain it to them in a thousand years. If you'll think hack, Henry. You'll recall I paid high in Rome to keep away from them, innocent though I was. No, Henry: it won't be the police."

With visible relief, Fisher sank back into his corner. But his expression changed when Merrill added, looking at him critically:

With visible relief, Fisher sank back into his corner.

"Not the police, but—you and me are alone here, Henry. I could break you in two with one hand, and throw the pieces out that window. That's what I ought to do, I guess. But I'm a tender-hearted man—on my way to be married. And it was a clever game, Henry, a clever game."

Fisher smiled wanly.

"Glad you appreciate it," he murmured.

"I'm no cry-baby," said Merrill. "You got my roll. That's about the end of it. I ain't sure I didn't have it coming to me, I was so all-fired stuck up over what you said about me as a judge of men. And the stick, you gave it to the one man you couldn't swindle. By Gad, Henry, you sure are full of humor"

"It enlivens my work—humor," admitted Fisher.

"Tell me all about it," demanded Merrill. "I ought to know: I paid high. That roll of plans, now—"

"Did you examine them?" asked Fisher. "Artistic work, if I do say it myself. Sat up in my cabin the last five nights working on them: the Champagne district as I think it ought to he."

"And the gent with the credentials who called on me in Rome? Come, Henry, tell me all about it. Remember how you used to tell me all your pranks? Who was he? What did you pay him?"

"An ex-guide," said Fisher. "These are dull days for guides. He did it for a hundred. He would have stuck a knife in you for less."

"A hundred lire," mused Merrill. "Good profits, Henry. Better than the cattle game. I wonder now, Henry, if you've got ten thousand lire about your lying, sneaking person—"

He stood over Fisher threateningly, but his late friend looked up at him without a trace of worry in his face.

"Look me over," he said. "I told you many times—it isn't my method to carry loot about on me. I've only got a little change. Those ten thousand are banked, old boy: banked where you'll never get them." He held up his arms. "Search me," he suggested.

"No use." Merrill shook his head. "Besides, I'm no pickpocket. Henry, it begins to look as though I'll just have to take my medicine and shut up. After all, I've got something out of the deal. I'll look out for the next man that batters me. What a convincing liar you are, my boy!"

"I'm sorry," replied Fisher. "Really, I am. An artist looks at a sunset, and he just has to paint it. I looked at you, and you called out to the artist in me. I had to do you."

"And you was just plain lying," mused Merrill. "All that about my being a great judge of men, and nobody could swindle me—"

"Well, it looks that way, doesn't it?"

"A lesson for me, Henry. I'll never get puffed up again. And—" he glanced toward the gold elephant above him— "there is a little something you can do for me, after all. You can make me a present all over again. You can give me that ebony stick to carry—so that I'll always be reminded I'm the easiest fool in shoe leather. You'll do that, Henry?"

Fisher's jaws set.

"I will not," he said. "That stick is mine. I need it." The ranchman came closer. "It's mine—let it alone,"

"My boy," said Merrill softly, "don't act up. I want that stick: I want it for a souvenir—a reminder—to keep me humble like I should be—"

"Let it alone!" Fisher screamed. He started to rise from his seat, when suddenly the huge fingers of the ranchman's left hand engulfed his throat. He did not speak again, but the shifty eyes that looked up at Merrill filled suddenly with a deep respect.

"Boy," said Merrill, "I could break you in two. Don't rile me. It ain't much I ask, just the ebony stick—"

"All right," gurgled Fisher, and Merrill let go. "I'm full of that humor you spoke of. Poetic justice. I suppose it is." His face was bitter as he reached up and secured the stick. "Take it—from your old friend Fisher." He sneered, with a low bow.

"To the easiest mark you ever met," smiled Merrill.

"No!" snarled Fisher. "No! The old presentation speech still stands."

Merrill paused a second, thoughtfully.

"I'll be going hack to my second-class corner," he said. "The high grade company in this red plush compartment ain't to my liking."

He went out into the corridor, grasping his prize. Fisher followed him to the door. "Damn you!" he cried. "Why didn't you stick to that Cook's schedule? I banked on it. I said nothing on God's green earth could switch you."

"From now on," Merrill answered, "nothing will. You've got my route, 1 guess, Don't get in my way again. Good-by."

In the corridor outside his own compartment he sought to spring the catch that should open the head of the stick but, ignorant of the secret, his efforts were in vain. In another moment he was surrounded by a restless crowd bearing luggage, and an officer of whom he had made inquiries earlier in the journey tapped him on the shoulder.

"Firenze," said the Italian.

"By golly, he means Florence." Merrill cried, and his thoughts were no longer of walking sticks as he dove in to get his baggage.

Florence proved to be the most lovely of all cities, for Celia Ware was waiting on the platform. A trifle more mature, a trifle wiser in the world's ways than when she left Texas to win fame and fortune, she seemed standing there; but still the Celia of the joyous eyes, the heart-warming smile. Bob Merrill overturned citizens to reach her side.

"Celia," he cried. "Let me hear you say it. You want me more than music— "

She clutched his arm.

"Oh, Bob," she answered. "You mean more than Beethoven to me."

The glory of this renunciation caught Merrill in the throat, and without more preamble he took her in his arms and kissed her. The Italians are an emotional people, and the scene was not unappreciated.

They were married next day in the English Church of the Holy Trinity, and in the crowded, gorgeous time that followed Merrill thought little of the ebony stick, save once when he humbly related his adventure to his wife. Italy decked itself in the glad habiliments of summer for their honeymoon; the sea was glittering glass when they sailed over it for home. The last week in July brought them, happy, once more to the Silver Star.

On a certain very hot morning early in August Clay Garrett opened the door of that Texas bank as the clock on the City Hall struck nine. Two minutes later, according to his custom, Major Tellfair entered, nodded to Clay and the boys, and passed on into his office. Another five minutes elapsed, and Bob Merrill, with the family smile on his face, strode into that marble interior, an ebony stick in his hand.

Major Tellfair rose quickly in welcome as Merrill entered the president's office. Certain formalities about the day and the Silver Star being disposed of, Merrill held up his walking stick. "Major," he said? "I told you the story of how I came by this cane. I reckon you remember—"

"Of course I do," said the major."

And I'm eternally sorry that I left you waiting over there in Rome—"

"Best thing you ever did," Merrill interrupted. "I reckon I forgot to mention that when that low-down rascal gave me this stick the second time, as per my warm request, he said: 'The old presentation speech still stands.' I didn't gather what he meant at the time, but do now. Major, sir—there's been a sequel—and a dog-goned nice sequel, too."

"Indeed, sir, I am very glad to hear it."

"You know, l was so all-fired taken with the joys of matrimony I didn't pay any attention to this stick coming home. But last night out at the ranch got to fooling with it, and the handle came off." Merrill reached into his pocket, and threw down a small bundle of thin paper before his friend. "Major, as my banker, what am I going to do with that truck?"

"Last night out at the ranch got to fooling with it, and the handle came off."

"Ah—um—" Major Tellfair studied the roll. "These seem to be banknotes issued in Italy, each for a thousand lire—"

"Correct," laughed Merrill. "And there's ten of them—ten nice new notes for a thousand lire each—the identical ten I handed over to a greasy little Dago in the Bank Ditallyuh, or whatever you call it. That slick Fisher told me they was banked where I'd never get them, but he was wrong—dead wrong."

He leaned buck in his chair and laughed again.

"Major, I'm a happy man. I'm married to the finest girl in Texas—and that means the world. And I went up against the slickest con man on the Seven Seas, and l did him. Yes, sir; l did him out of the hundred lire he paid that guy to get me."

"I'm delighted," beamed the major. "That was a lucky meeting of yours: that second one with Fisher. It begins to look like my boy Clay burst into song at just the right date and locality."

"That's true," agreed Merrill. "I'd almost forgotten that. Yes, sir—Clay surely launched into 'Silver Threads Among the Gold' at what they call the psychological moment. By the way, how about this stuff?"

"I'll send it to New York to-day," the major promised, "and have it translated into real money for you. I won't forget, Bob."

Merrill rose. "Thanks," he said. "Just put it to my account, major. I'm a happy man. But I mustn't get stuck on myself: that was the way I got done before."

He returned to the banking room; Clay Garrett was loafing amiably near the door. Merrill removed a roll of bills from his pocket, took a twenty-dollar note from the top, and pressed it into the negro's hand.

"That's yours, Clay." he said.

Clay staggered weakly. "Fo' de Lawd's sake, Mistuh Bob, what's this?"

"Just a few lire for you, Clay—that's all," Merrill answered.

"Liar?" What yo-all mean—liar? Mistuh Bob, I swear I ain't—"

"No offense," laughed Merrill. "I just want you to have it, Clay. I like your singing."

He went out into the street, leaving a dazed but happy negro leaning unsteadily against a marble post.

THE END

www.ingramcontent.com/pod-product-compliance
Lightning Source LLC
Chambersburg PA
CBHW030240180626
46810CB00008B/3228